CLARABEL

The Fat
Controller
says...

Suitable for babies from
6 months

No added preservatives

No artificial sweeteners

No colours

Made with real fruit purée

No fruit bits

Suitable for vegetarians

St Michael

THOMAS
THE TANK ENGINE
& FRIENDS ™

APPLE DRINK

NO ADDED SUGAR
30% FRUIT JUICE
250 ml e

St Michael

THOMAS
THE TANK ENGINE
& FRIENDS ™

APPLE DRINK

NO ADDED SUGAR
30% FRUIT JUICE
250 ml e

Henry
AND THE GHOST TRAIN

by Christopher Awdry

illustrated by Ken Stott

Heinemann • London

First published in Great Britain 1993
by William Heinemann Ltd, an imprint of
Reed Children's Books Ltd,
Michelin House, 81 Fulham Road, London SW3 6RB
AUCKLAND · MELBOURNE · SINGAPORE · TORONTO

Copyright © William Heinemann Ltd 1993

ISBN 0 434 96399 2

Printed in Great Britain

A fair had come to the Island of Sodor. Men had set up
stalls and rides near the junction. A notice on one
of them said it was a GHOST TRAIN.

"What is a ghost train?" Daisy asked her driver.
"It is a tunnel that trains run through," he explained,
"past skeletons and ghosts and other spooky things."

Henry was at the next platform. He saw Daisy shiver.
"Pooh!" he scoffed. "I'm not scared - only silly little
engines are frightened of ghosts." And he puffed away.

At the big station everyone was talking about ghosts.
"I'm not scared of stupid old ghosts," Henry said.
But he did not want to meet one, just in case ...

That evening Henry's driver told him: "Part of the
tunnel roof has collapsed. The Fat Controller says we
must take some men to clear away the rubble."

"Bother," grumbled Henry. "I was looking forward to a rest."
"Cheer up, Henry," said his driver. "Pushing trucks into
a tunnel does not sound very much like hard work to me."

Still grumbling, Henry pushed two trucks and a van full of workmen into the tunnel. They filled the trucks with rubble and Henry began to pull them out again.

He was going nicely when suddenly there was a loud clanking noise.
"Your tender is off the line," said his driver.

"We must have run into some rubble. We can't go forward and we can't go back. We shall have to wait until the Fat Controller can sort something out."

It was very quiet in the tunnel. The workmen walked home and Henry dozed, but he woke up with a start. He was moving!

"Ooooooooooooh . . . er!" wailed a ghostly voice a
a white shape floated towards him.
Henry was terrified.

Henry was icy cold and his wheels were shaking, but
he hurried on. Suddenly something strange fluttered in front
of him, moaning and groaning.

Everywhere big eyes were staring at him out of the darkness.

"Peeeep peeeep," he whistled loudly. "Help me!"

Then Henry saw a station ahead. He felt much
better now. He slowed down to stop, but when he saw
what was on the platform he did not want to!

The station had a skeleton staff and a Very Thin Controller. And waiting to catch the train was a vampire!

When he heard "poooop poooop" in the distance,
Henry felt better.
"That sounds like Gordon," he said.

But it was a ghostly, shadowy Gordon who rushed towards him with a scream and a roar.

Just as Henry felt he could bear no more, he heard his driver's voice.

"Wake up, Henry," the driver said. "Your tender
is back on the line. We can go home now."

Henry was delighted. He went quickly back to the
shed and had a long drink of water. He felt
better after that.

But he was careful not to tell the other engines about the Ghost Train. He was sure they would laugh at him.